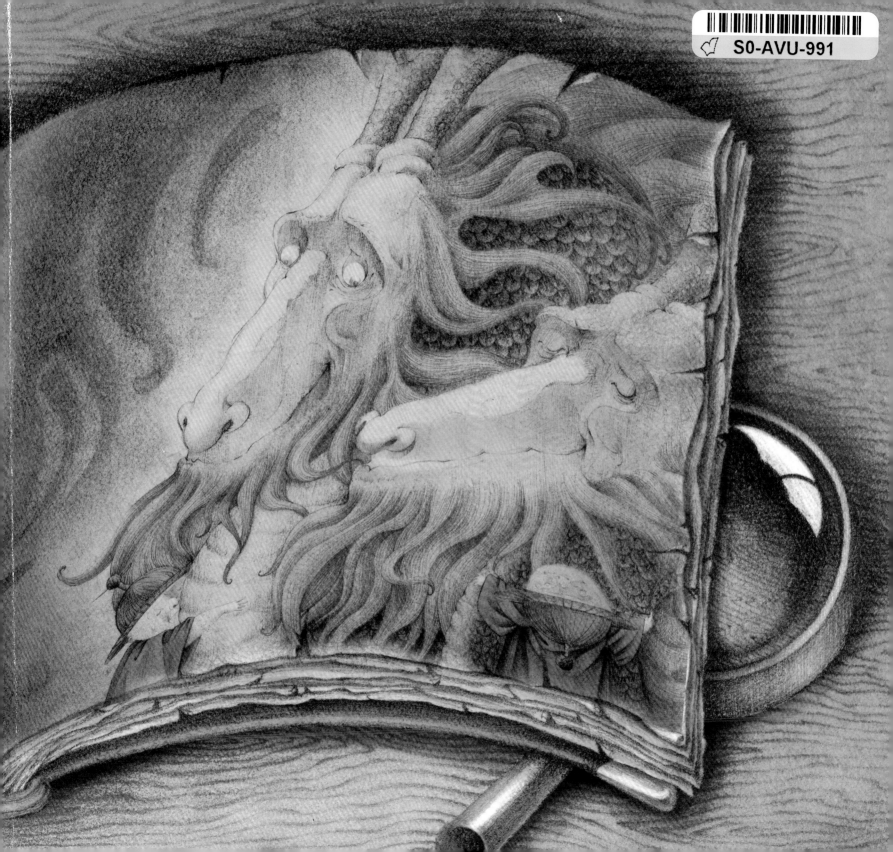

The Dragon Tribe

Published by:
Better Chinese LLC
P.O.Box 695
Palo Alto, CA 94302
Tel: (650) 384-0902
Email: usa@betterchinese.com
Web: www.BetterChinese.com

Library of Congress Cataloging-in-Publication Data

Xiong, Kim, 1975-
    [Tu long zhu. English]
    The Dragon Tribe / by Kim Xiong ; translated by Clarissa Yu Shen ; [illustrated by the QiYuBaoTongShu Workshop].
    p.cm.
    Summary: Tells the story of how the Dragon Slayers in ancient China became known simply as the Dragon Tribe.
    IBN-13: 978-1-60603-000-4 (hardcover : alk. paper)
    ISBN-10: 1-60603-000-0 (hardcover : alk. paper) [1. Dragons--Fiction. 2. China--History--Fiction.] I. Shen, Clarissa Yu, 1977- II. QiYuBaoTongShu Workshop (Firm) III. Title.

    PZ7.X53Dr 2008
    [E]-dc22

2008030276

奇界堡童书出品

www.BetterChinese.com

The Dragon Tribe

KIM XIONG
Translated by Clarissa Yu Shen

Once upon a time, in the middle of the middle kingdom, lived a tribe known as the Dragon Slayers.

They were a rare people and little has been written about them.

They were also a small tribe
because they had few children.
It was a rough world they lived in.

But the children they did have were brave and strong.

Each child could kill a dragon before they grew their first beard,

proving themselves as Dragon Slayers.

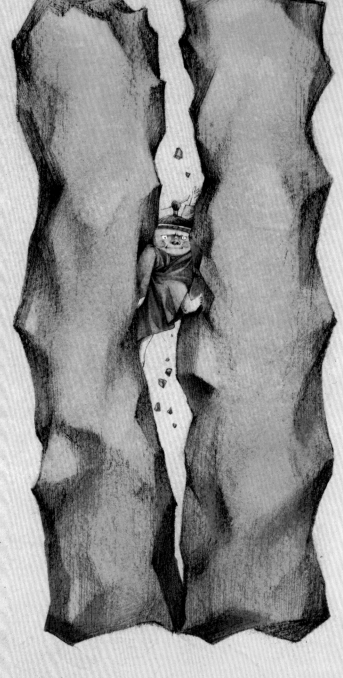

And the children would seek out dragons everywhere: in the depths of the ocean,

in hard to reach nooks and crannies,

up in the heavens,   leaving no stone unturned.

Over time, dragons became harder and harder to find.
Some children even grew long beards before they saw their first dragon.

And one day, when a child asked, "Baba, what is a dragon?"
the Dragon Slayers knew they had to do something.
How could they be known as the Dragon Slayers if their
children no longer knew what dragons were?

So it was that the elders started to paint, and sculpt,
and write beautiful stories and poems about dragons.
Their children would know how great those dragons were!

Over the years, their children played with dragon toys, wore dragon-embroidered clothing, and heard dragon story after dragon story.

To find a dragon became every child's dream.

But would they ever find a dragon?

A few of the most courageous children continued to search...

… up high, higher than even the clouds…

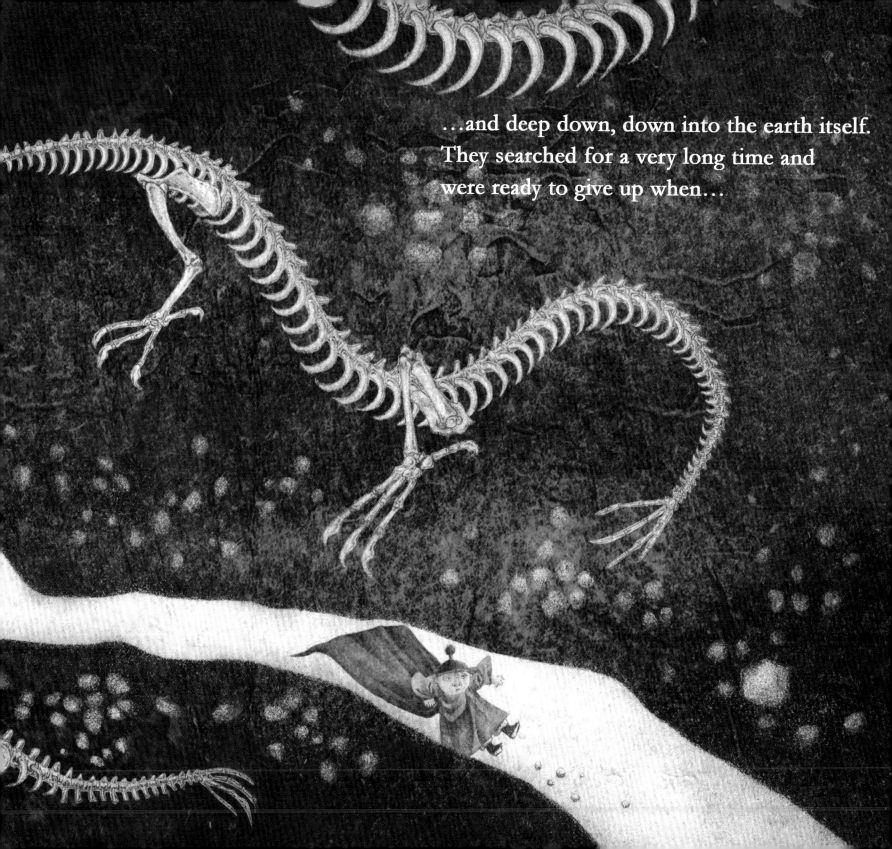

…and deep down, down into the earth itself.
They searched for a very long time and
were ready to give up when…

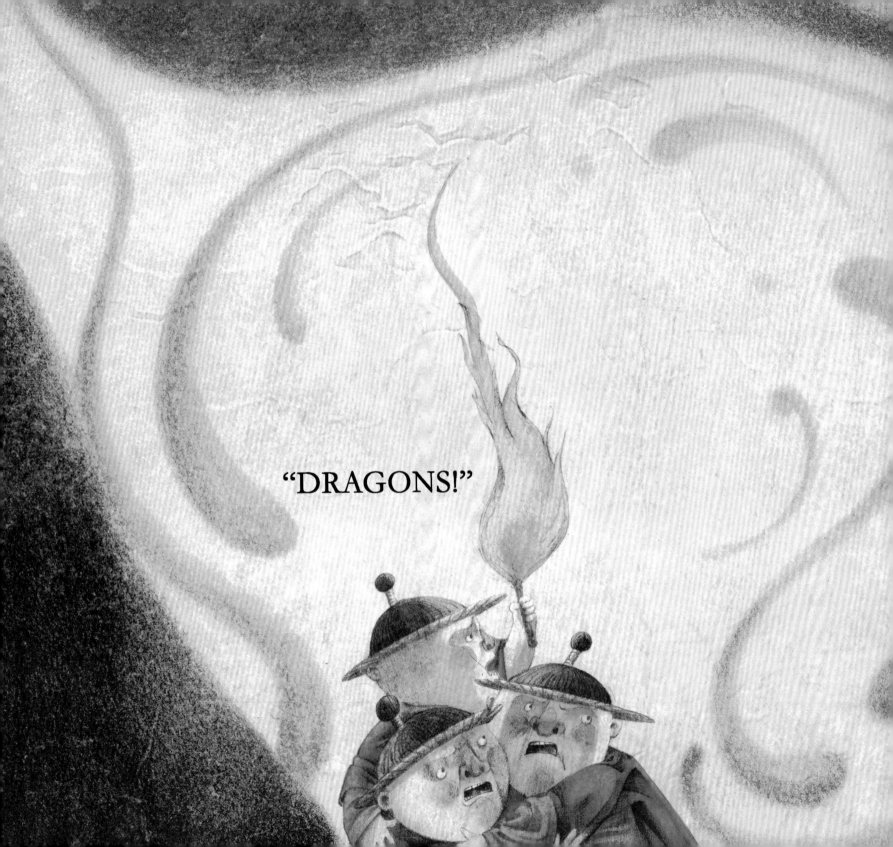

"DRAGONS!"

But these children no longer wanted to kill dragons.
After all the stories they had heard, the children now
loved these magical creatures.

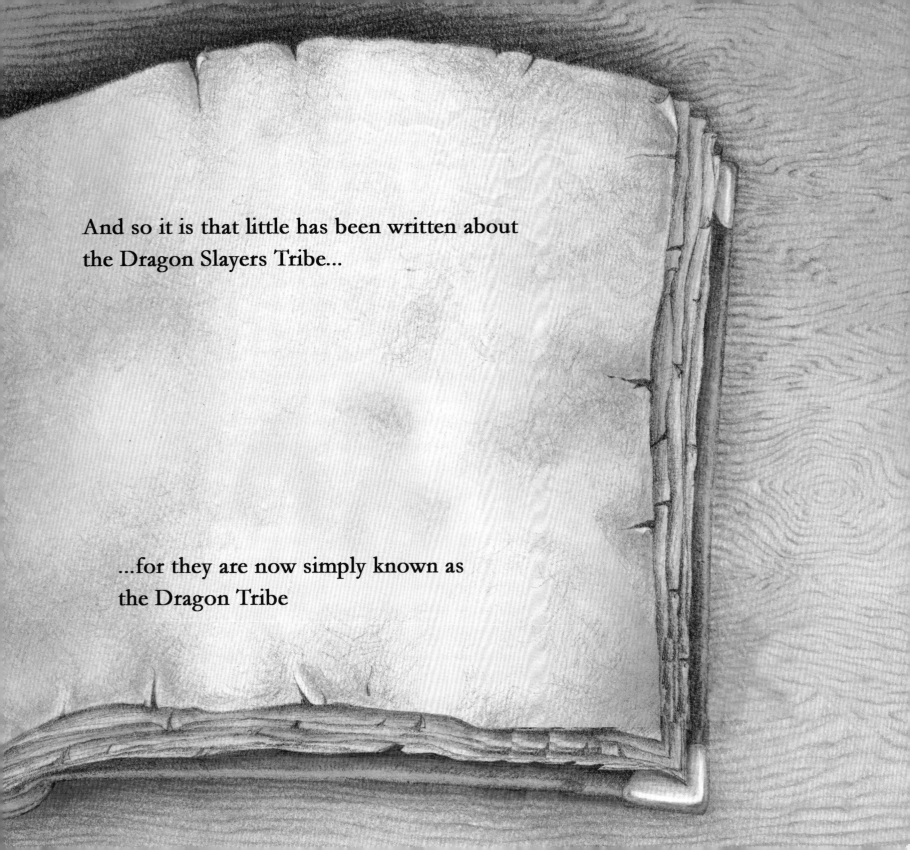

And so it is that little has been written about
the Dragon Slayers Tribe...

...for they are now simply known as
the Dragon Tribe

tú lóng zú
屠 龙 族

hěn jiǔ hěn jiǔ yǐ qián　　yǒu yì zú rén　　tā men jiào tú lóng yì zú
很 久 很 久 以 前 ，　有 一 族 人 ，　他 们 叫 屠 龙 一 族 。

tā men zhè gè mín zú de rén fēi cháng shǎo　　suǒ yǐ wǒ men duì tā men de liǎo jiě yě
他 们 这 个 民 族 的 人 非 常 少 ，　所 以 我 们 对 他 们 的 了 解 也

fēi cháng fēi cháng shǎo
非 常 非 常 少 。

tā men de rén shù zhī suǒ yǐ hěn shǎo　　shì yīn wèi tā men suǒ shēng xià de měi yí gè
他 们 的 人 数 之 所 以 很 少 ，　是 因 为 他 们 所 生 下 的 每 一 个

hái zi dōu xū yào jīng guò jīng tiāo xì xuǎn　　bú gòu qiáng zhuàng　　bú gòu yǒng gǎn de
孩 子 都 需 要 经 过 精 挑 细 选 。　不 够 强 壮 、　不 够 勇 敢 的

dōu yào bèi diū qì
都 要 被 丢 弃 。

shèng xià de měi yí gè hái zi dōu bèi jīng xīn de péi yǎng chéng tú lóng dòu shì　　tā men
剩 下 的 每 一 个 孩 子 都 被 精 心 地 培 养 成 屠 龙 斗 士 。　他 们

dōu yǐ shā sǐ lóng wéi zì jǐ de jiāo ào
都 以 杀 死 龙 为 自 己 的 骄 傲 。

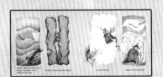

tā men bù tíng de zhǎo lóng tiǎo zhàn　　zài shēn shēn de hǎi dǐ　　zài dì dǐ de liè fèng
他 们 不 停 地 找 龙 挑 战 ，　在 深 深 的 海 底 ，　在 地 底 的 裂 缝

lǐ　　zài gāo gāo de tiān shàng　　rèn hé dì fang dōu bú huì fàng guò
里 ，　在 高 高 的 天 上 …… 任 何 地 方 都 不 会 放 过 ！